FELA KUTI
Rebellious Father of Afrobeat

Written by Omenka Ulonka & Kaja Gulankaja

Illustrated by Omenka Ulonka (Ebele Okoye)

THiS BOOK BELONGS TO:

____

Age: _______________________

1

2

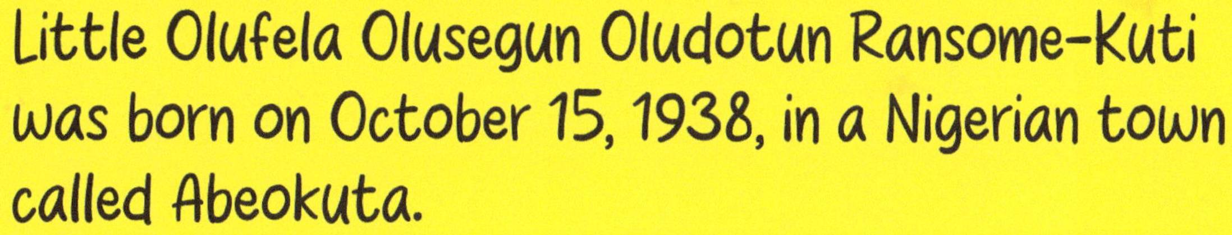

Little Olufela Olusegun Oludotun Ransome-Kuti was born on October 15, 1938, in a Nigerian town called Abeokuta.

His dad was a pastor and a teacher.
His mum, Funmilayo, was a very brave woman.
She worked hard so that girls and women
could have the same rights as boys and men.

Funmilayo was the first Nigerian woman to drive a car. Because of his mom, Olufela learned to be brave too. He later became a rebel, just like her.

Olufela was very curious about music.

So, he learned to play the piano, drums, and other instruments.

Olufela could also sing very well. So, when he was in school, he became the leader of the school choir.

When he grew up, his parents sent him to London to study medicine, but he did not like that. Instead he decided to study music.

His favourite instrument at the time was the trumpet. Because of that, he fell in love with jazz.

13

The next year, Olufela made his own band called "Fela Kuti and the Highlife Rakers."

From then on, people started
calling him Fela Kuti.

Fela created a new kind of music.

He combined many music styles with traditional
Yoruba music from Nigeria and called it "Afrobeat".

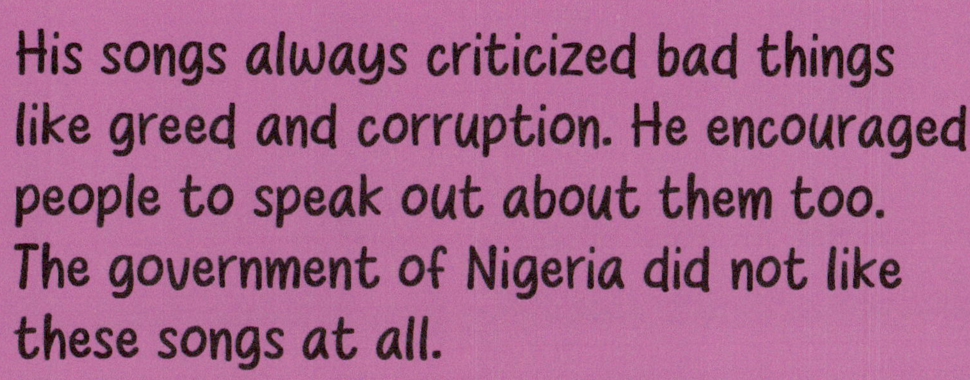

His songs always criticized bad things like greed and corruption. He encouraged people to speak out about them too. The government of Nigeria did not like these songs at all.

ARMY

So, Fela always got in
trouble with them.
They arrested him
200 times

Despite these, Fela never stopped
playing his music. He remained
brave and kept singing for change,
wanting to make the world a
better place.
In 1985, an organisation called
Amnesty International gave him
the name "Prisoner of Conscience"

On August 2, 1997, Fela Kuti died in a prison in Lagos, Nigeria. He made 50 albums when he was alive.

Even though he is dead, people remember and celebrate him every year, and his children Femi and Seun continue to play his music.

Ready For Some Colouring Fun?

You can download FREE colouring pages of this book from our website

https://spunkytoonz.com

You can also simply scan the QR code below to download.

But that's not all!
This book "Fela Kuti – Rebellious Father of Afrobeat'
is just one of our exciting book series
"Spunky Toonz Heroes, Icons, and Rebels."
Make sure to check out the others
for more inspiring stories of brave people
who have done wonderful things!

IMPRINT

Published by Spunky Toonz Ltd, Nigeria
Authors: Omenka Ulonka & Kaja Gulankaja
Illustrator: Omenka Ulonka
Copyright © 2024 Spunky Toonz Ltd.

ISBN: 978-3-911413-00-8

www.ingramcontent.com/pod-product-compliance
Lightning Source LLC
LaVergne TN
LVHW071617180726

843512LV00003B/662